Grimm's
Fairy Tales

For Auntie Maria
S.P.

For Tim
C.J.

ORCHARD BOOKS
338 Euston Road, London NW1 3BH
Orchard Books Australia
Level 17/207 Kent Street, Sydney, NSW 2000

This text was first published in the form of a gift collection called
The Sleeping Princess by Orchard Books in 2002

This edition first published in hardback in 2012
First paperback publication in 2013

ISBN 978 1 40830 831 8 (hardback)
ISBN 978 1 40830 832 5 (paperback)

Text © Saviour Pirotta 2002
Illustrations © Cecilia Johansson 2012

The rights of Saviour Pirotta to be identified as the author and
Cecilia Johansson to be identified as the illustrator of this work
have been asserted by them in accordance
with the Copyright, Designs and Patents Act, 1988.

A CIP catalogue record for this book is available
from the British Library.

1 3 5 7 9 10 8 6 4 2 (hardback)
1 3 5 7 9 10 8 6 4 2 (paperback)

Printed in China

Orchard Books is a division of Hachette Children's Books,
an Hachette UK company.
www.hachette.co.uk

Grimm's Fairy Tales

Hansel and Gretel

Written by Saviour Pirotta
Illustrated by Cecilia Johansson

ORCHARD

Once there was a woodcutter who had two
children, a boy called Hansel and a girl
called Gretel. He loved them very much, but
his wife – their stepmother – didn't like
them at all.

One winter, the cold weather ruined the crops. Everyone in the land was going hungry.

"Why don't we take Hansel and Gretel deep into the forest and leave them there?" suggested his wife one night. "That'll be two less mouths to feed."

The woodcutter was horrified. What a thing to suggest! But his wife went on arguing and badgering until he said yes.

The poor man went to bed with a great sadness in his heart.

Hansel and Gretel were still awake, because their tummies were rumbling with hunger. They heard every single word their cruel stepmother said.

Hansel comforted Gretel and said, "Don't worry. We'll find our way back somehow."

When the house was quiet, Hansel crept downstairs to the garden and filled his pockets with lots of tiny white stones.

The next morning, the four set off towards the forest. In front was the woodcutter's wife, then the woodcutter who held hands with Gretel. Last of all came Hansel, dropping the white stones from his pockets as he walked.

When they reached the middle of the forest, the woodcutter built a fire and settled his children down beside it.

"Now rest, my little ones," he said, "your stepmother and I are going to chop some wood."

Hansel and Gretel sat by the fire and ate their lunch. They were not at all scared, for they could hear their father chopping wood nearby. After a while, they fell asleep.

When they woke it was dark and no one was there. Gretel trembled.

"Look, there are my stones shining in the moonlight," said Hansel . . .

. . . and they followed the trail of pebbles all the way back home.

Their stepmother was furious but the woodcutter hugged his children close.

Food was still scarce, so a short time later, the stepmother started to complain again. Once more, the woodcutter didn't want to let his children go, but his wife wore him down.

When the lights were out, Hansel crept downstairs once more to fetch some stones.

But this time his stepmother had locked the door. Hansel returned to bed with empty pockets.

In the morning, the children were given
a hunk of bread and led into the forest.

Hansel, not having any stones, left a trail
of breadcrumbs behind him instead.

The children helped their father light a fire and, before long, they fell asleep.

When they woke up, it was dark and the owls were hooting. Their parents had left.

"Don't worry, Gretel," said Hansel. "We'll follow the trail of breadcrumbs to get home."

But the birds had eaten up all the bread! There was no trail. The children were completely lost.

All night long they wandered through
the forest . . . until they came
to a little cottage.

What a delicious house it was! The walls were made of gingerbread, the roof of cake and chocolate, and the windowpanes of spun sugar!

Hansel tore off a part of the roof, while Gretel broke off a piece of windowpane.

"Who's nibbling at my house?" someone called, and an old woman came out. "Why, it's two hungry children," she said, her eyes twinkling. "Come inside, and I'll make you a proper meal."

Hansel and Gretel followed the old woman into the house.

The old woman might have looked harmless but really she was a wicked witch.

After the meal, she suggested Hansel and Gretel have a little sleep. Her bed looked so comfortable, the two of them climbed in.

Early next morning, the witch dragged Hansel out of bed and locked him in a cage!

Then she kicked Gretel awake and said,
"Light the fire, child – we're making some
porridge to fatten up your brother. When
he is nice and plump I shall roast him and
eat him!"

Gretel was given only scraps to eat, while
Hansel was fed all kinds of delicious food.

Every day, the witch went up to the cage
and said, "Stretch out a finger, you little brat.
Let's see if my food is making you fat."

Hansel, who knew the witch could not see very well, would stick a chicken bone through the bars.

"Pah," grumbled the witch. "Still not plump enough."

After four weeks, the witch got tired of waiting. "Gretel," she called, "check the oven. See if it is hot enough."

"Aha," thought Gretel, "she means to lock me in the oven and cook me." So she said, "But how do I get in to check?"

"For goodness' sake," snapped the witch. "You must climb in like this." And she got down on all fours to show Gretel.

Gretel gave the witch a mighty
push and she tumbled head
first into the fire.

Then Gretel set her brother free and the two of them hugged and danced.

Then they filled their pockets with pearls and jewels from the witch's treasure and ran all the way home.

There they found their father sitting at the kitchen table. His wife had died, and he was all alone. Hansel and Gretel ran to him and hugged and kissed him.

Then they emptied out their pockets until the table was covered in pearls and jewels.

"We shall never be poor or hungry again,"
said Gretel, and the three of them lived
together in perfect happiness.